MEXICO
WORLD ADVENTURES
BY STEFFI CAVELL-CLARKE

BookLife

©2016
Book Life
King's Lynn
Norfolk PE30 4LS

ISBN: 978-1-78637-008-2

Written by:
Steffi Cavell-Clarke
Designed by:
Natalie Carr

A catalogue record for this book
is available from the British Library.

MEXICO
WORLD ADVENTURES

Words in **bold** can be found in the glossary on page 24.

CONTENTS

WHERE IS MEXICO?

AMERICA

MEXICO

Mexico is a country in the southern part of North America. The capital city of Mexico is called Mexico City.

MEXICO

The **population** in Mexico is over one hundred and twenty-two million. Most people who live in Mexico speak Spanish.

Mexico has a hot **climate** all year round. In the dry season, there is hardly any rain and the ground gets very dry.

There are lots of different landscapes in Mexico. It has hot, sandy deserts and high mountains. Mexico also has long stretches of beach.

SONORAN DESERT IN MEXICO

CLOTHING

People in Mexico mostly wear cool and comfortable clothing because of the hot climate.

A **traditional** hat in Mexico is called a Sombrero. This is a very large hat that protects the head, neck and shoulders from the sun.

SOMBRERO

RELIGION

The religion with the most followers in Mexico is Christianity. Most of the Christians are **Roman Catholic**.

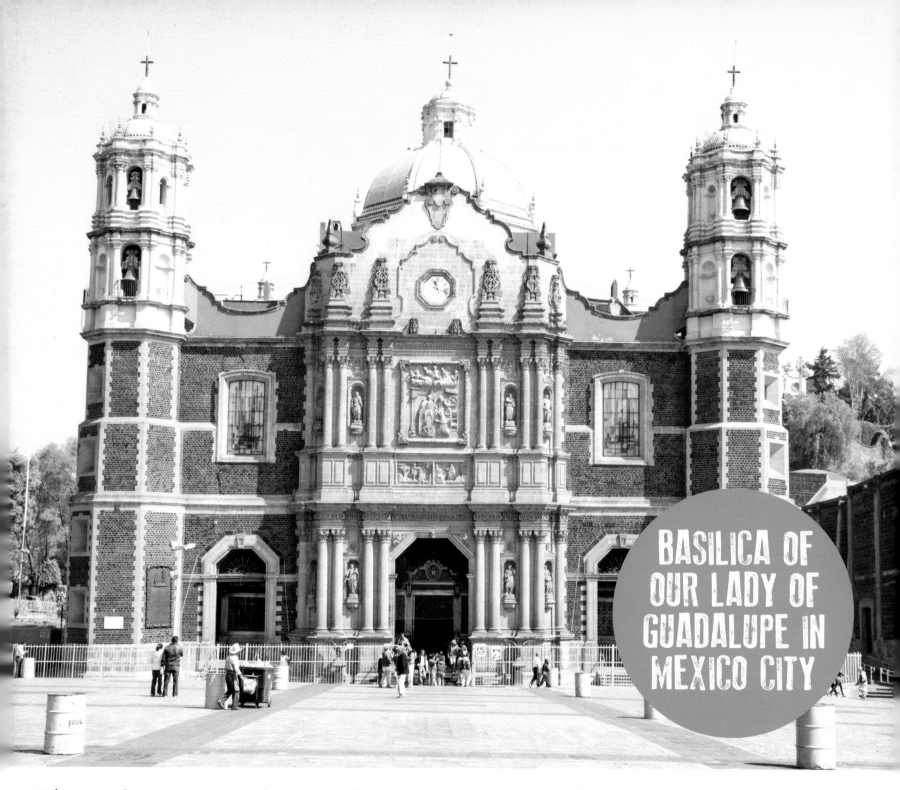

BASILICA OF
OUR LADY OF
GUADALUPE IN
MEXICO CITY

The Christian place of **worship** is a church. They visit the church every Sunday for prayer.

FOOD

SALSA

Mexican food can be very spicy. A traditional dish in Mexico are Nachos. Nachos are often dipped in a spicy sauce called Salsa.

Tortillas are very popular in Mexico. They are small pancakes made out of maize flour, and are often eaten with spicy food and sauces.

FRIED TORTILLAS ARE CALLED TACOS

AT SCHOOL

Children who go to school in Mexico study Spanish, maths, geography, science and history.

Children also play sport at school. They often play games like football where they learn how to play as a team.

AT HOME

In big cities in Mexico, many people live with their families in tall blocks of flats.

MODERN FLATS IN MEXICO CITY

Many families live on farms where they grow fruit and vegetables. Animals, such as donkeys, can also live on the farms.

FAMILIES

Most children in Mexico live with their **siblings** and parents. Many families live with other **relatives**, such as aunts, uncles, cousins and grandparents.

Families like to come together to celebrate special occasions, such as birthdays. Children like to play the piñata game at parties.

Children take turns to hit the piñata to get to the sweets inside.

SPORT

The most popular sport in Mexico is football. Lots of children play football after school and watch their favourite teams on television.

NETTED HOOP

Basketball is also a popular sport in Mexico. Two teams play aginst each other and each team tries to throw a ball through one of the netted hoops.

FUN FACTS

There are two **volcanoes** near Mexico City. They are called Popocateptl and Iztaccihuatl. The name Popocateptl means Smoking Mountain.

POPOCATEPTL IN MEXICO

RIO GRANDE IN MEXICO

The longest river in Mexico is called Rio Grande.
It is 1,896 miles long.

GLOSSARY

climate: the weather in a large area

population: amount of people living in a place

relatives: different people in a family

Roman Catholic: a type of Christianity

siblings: brothers and sisters

traditional: ways of behaving that have been done for a long time

volcanoes: a large mountain that has hot, melted rock inside.

worship: a religious act, such as praying

INDEX